MW00947968

This book is dedicated to:

Charlie,
for being a curious, encyclopedia loving,
animal and nature enthusiast, &
for inspiring me to begin writing children's books.

With thanks to:

Cubbie,
for supporting my crazy ideas.
Everyday and everywhere.
Love you!

Copyright © 2022
Red Ribbit Reads

www.redribbitreads.com
@redribbitreads

Written & designed by
Holly Moore

Illustrated by
Natalie Blazhievska

Title
Charlie Armadillo – National Parks Explorer
Channel Islands Surprise

Publisher's Cataloging-in-Publication data

Names: Moore, Holly, 1981-, author. | Blazhievska, Natalie, illustrator.
Title: Charlie Armadillo Channel Islands Surprise / written & designed by: Holly Moore; illustrated by: Natalie Blazhievska.
Series: Charlie Armadillo – National Parks Explorer
Description: Katy, TX: Red Ribbit Reads LLC, 2022. | Summary: Charlie and his family explore Anacapa Island in Channel Islands
National Park for a kid-friendly boat ride, hike, and unexpected quest to discover a critter unique to the island that Charlie has
never seen before.
Identifiers: LCCN: 2022935609 | ISBN: 979-8-9852702-8-0 (hardcover) |
979-8-9852702-7-3 (paperback) | 979-8-9852702-9-7 (eBook)
Subjects: LCSH Armadillos--Juvenile fiction. | Anacapa Island (Calif.)--Juvenile fiction. | Channel Islands (Calif.)--Juvenile fiction. |
Channel Islands National Park (Calif.)--Juvenile fiction. | BISAC JUVENILE FICTION / Travel | JUVENILE FICTION / People & Places
/ United States / General | JUVENILE FICTION / Animals / General
Classification: LCC PZ7.1 .M66 Cha 2022 | DDC [E]--dc23

All rights reserved. No part of this publication may be
reproduced or transmitted in any form without prior
written permission from the author.

CharLie ArmadiLlo
National Parks ExpLorer

CHANNEL ISLANDS
SURPRISE

Channel Islands
National Park

Written & Designed by
Holly Moore

Illustrated by
Natalie Blazhievska

For as long as he could remember, Charlie Armadillo wanted to be an EXPLORER.

He loved animals and nature.

He had practically memorized his National Parks encyclopedia and he felt like his brain was bursting with information!

Deep down, Charlie knew a real explorer needed to get outside to make discoveries!

As a member of the Kids in Nature Discovery Club, Charlie was determined to live up to his KIND Club pledge everyday.

Charlie couldn't wait for Sunday. His family was taking a boat to **Channel Islands National Park** to explore Anacapa Island.

He loved visiting National Parks! He felt like a real explorer, and there was plenty of wildlife to discover.

He tried to find one animal that was special to each National Park. Charlie appreciated the parks more and more with each adventure.

What discoveries would Charlie make on Anacapa?

He had never been to an island, but he'd read they were unique habitats for some animals.
On the boat, Charlie strapped on his life vest and found a seat.

He was hoping to catch a glimpse of a **humpback whale!**

The boat zoomed across the ocean. Charlie held
tight to the railing as something sailed out
of the water and dove back in with a

S-P-L-A-S-H-!!!

Charlie added "dolphin" to his KIND
Club Animal Tracker.
Not my humpback, Charlie grinned,
but I'll take it

In the distance, Charlie could see Channel Islands. This was going to be an exciting day!

When they reached the dock, Charlie couldn't believe his eyes!

The cliffs of Anacapa were so much

than they seemed in his encyclopedia!

He huffed and puffed his way to the top. Armadillos were not great at climbing stairs.

A Park Ranger handed Charlie a Junior Ranger packet as he soaked in the scenery.

He definitely needed to add "seagulls" to his tracker — he'd never seen so many at once!

ANACAPA ISLAND

As his parents wandered ahead, a fuzzy grey blur skittered across Charlie's path.

Before he could get a good look, the critter disappeared into a bush!

Charlie thought about the animals he'd expected to find in Channel Islands National Park.

Townsend's Big-eared Bat?

Allen's hummingbird?

Island Spotted Skunk?

There were no fuzzy grey animals that he could think of.

Had he just seen
– and lost –
his special Anacapa animal?

Charlie's tummy growled
as the Armadillos reached an overlook.

Cathedral
Cove

He dug a snack out of his backpack.

Who doesn't love
ants on a log?

(He didn't add "ants" to his tracker
though – that would be cheating.)
As he ate, he kept his eyes peeled for
something little and quick.

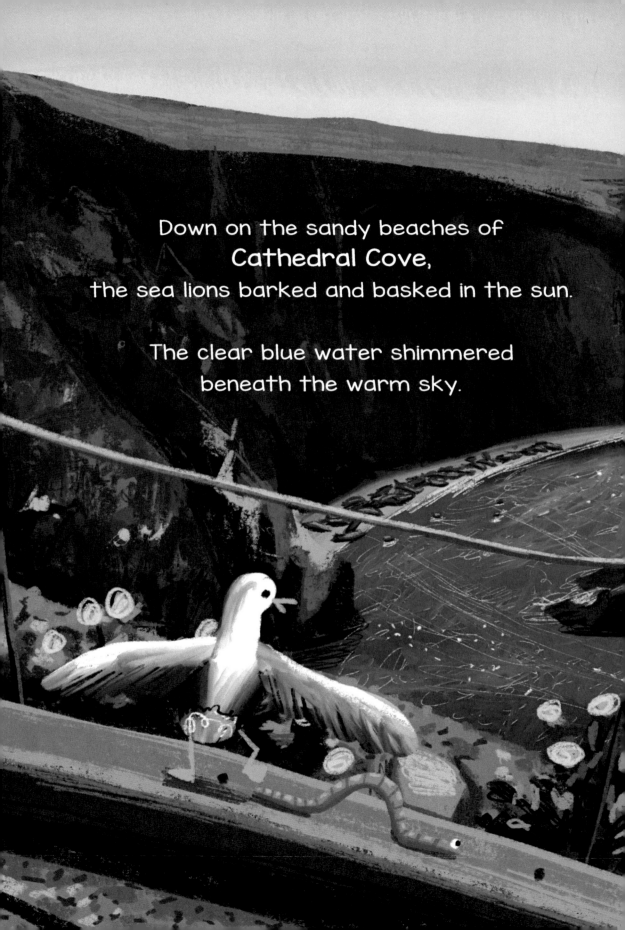

Down on the sandy beaches of
Cathedral Cove,
the sea lions barked and basked in the sun.

The clear blue water shimmered
beneath the warm sky.

Charlie added "sea lions" to his tracker.
The sea lions were definitely not his
mystery animal.

They weren't
little or quick.
They were loud
and lazy!

Up the trail, Inspiration Point
looked just like Charlie's favorite
picture from his encyclopedia.

He looked across to the other islands.
If something little and quick was over
there, it was too far away to tell.

Channel Islands National Park
was beautiful — but where was
his unique animal?

His goal of finding a special animal
was starting to feel ...

I–M–P–O–S–S–I–B–L–E.

Charlie was determined to look harder.
The seagulls squawked and gave him funny
looks as he strolled by.

He was fairly certain they hadn't seen an
armadillo on the island before.

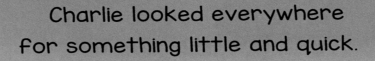

Charlie looked everywhere
for something little and quick.

He
checked
to the
right.

He
checked
to the
left.

He looked UP ... and DOWN

the
lighthouse
walls.

He looked around
BIG rocks ...

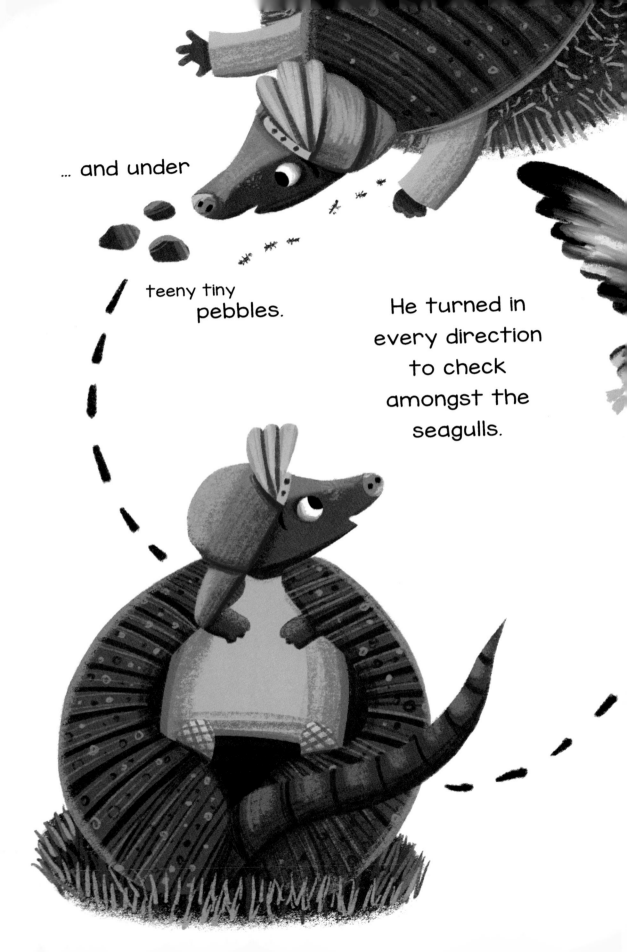

... and under

teeny tiny
pebbles.

He turned in
every direction
to check
amongst the
seagulls.

He even checked his backpack,
just in case.

Finally, Charlie peered behind a
bush — and saw a pair of bulging
eyes staring back at him.

It looked like a MOUSE!

The mouse skittered next to some
eggs in a seagull nest. It was little, and
it was quick!

Charlie was sure it was his mystery critter!

mouse

He added "mouse" to his tracker, though he was somewhat puzzled over his discovery. He hadn't read about mice on Anacapa in his encyclopedia.

Before long, it was time for Charlie
and his family to head home.
Charlie suddenly remembered the
packet the Park Ranger had given him!

He needed to finish the activities in it to
earn his Junior Ranger badge.

A smile spread across
Charlie's face as he read.
~ TEN THOUSAND ~
seagulls came to Anacapa to
lay their eggs each summer.

Channel Islands National Park sure was a
special place for seagulls!

Finishing his word search, Charlie

OOOOHed

out loud as he read the next page.

Name: Charlie

CHANNEL ISLANDS WORD SEARCH

```
    U  S  M  V  W  V  Z  B  Y  X  S     A
    P  E  L  I  C  A  N  T  C  C  N     N
    F  A  J  K  E  Q  H  I  K  E  O     A
    O  L  D  O  L  P  H  I  N  I  R     C
    X  I  V  W  T  K  A  Y  A  K  K     A
    U  O  D  E  E  R  M  O  U  S  E     P
    V  N  E  X  P  L  O  R  E  I  L     A
    C  A  M  P  N  A  T  U  R  E  S     S
```

Find the following words in the puzzle.
Good Luck Junior Ranger!

ANACAPA   FOX   SEA LION
CAMP   HIKE   SNORKEL
DEER MOUSE   KAYAK   EXPLORE
DOLPHIN   NATURE   PELICAN

He spotted a familiar grey shape with
bulging black eyes and big ears.

The packet said it was the
island deer mouse,
a species that lived only on Anacapa Island.

Meet the Channel
Islands Deer Mouse!

They eats bugs
and seeds

★ Each island
has a unique
deer mouse

Charlie
circled the
unique
mouse on
his tracker.

Bingo! A new discovery from a
budding young explorer.

Charlie raced to tell
the Park Ranger what
he'd seen.

The Ranger pinned a
shiny badge
on his shirt and told him how lucky he'd
been to spot an island deer mouse!

They were little, and they were quick!

Charlie thought about his KIND Club
pledge and all the animals he'd seen.

He was
accomplishing
his dreams,
one discovery
at a time.

He imagined being

H–O–M–E.

He couldn't wait to scratch Channel Islands off of his KIND Club National Parks poster.

His badge glimmered in the sunlight as the
boat carried him back towards the coast.

No humpbacks this time, Charlie thought

But he didn't mind.

Today, he was a real EXPLORER.

K.I.N.D. Club
Fact Tracker
Channel Islands National Park

🏔️ Location — 5 islands off the Southern California coast (Anacapa, Santa Cruz, Santa Rosa, San Miguel, & Santa Barbara)

🏔️ The island deer mouse is one of 5 sub-species of deer mice found only in the Channel Islands.

🏔️ The vast majority of western seagulls are hatched on Anacapa Island!

🏔️ The island fox is the largest land mammal found on the islands. They have no predators, so they are out and about during daylight hours! But … you won't spot an island fox on Anacapa!

🏔️ The waters of Channel Islands serve as a migratory pathway for humpback whales in the late spring! Grey whales, pilot whales, fin whales, blue whales, and orcas, dolphins, and other porpoises are common to the Channel Islands.

🏔️ Channel Islands became a National Park & Marine Sanctuary in 1980

Will you spot a whale …
before Charlie does?

🏔️ Facts from NPS, Visit Ventura, See California, & other reputable sites

Did you L—O—V—E Charlie Armadillo?

If so, please use the QR code below to leave a review on Amazon!

Visit www.redribbitreads.com to find other books I have published, and/or www.charliearmadillo.com to check out fun facts about each Park Charlie has visited, and the trip gallery that inspires his stories!

Happy hiking ya'll!
Holly

Made in the USA
Las Vegas, NV
04 December 2024

13364310R00026